This edition published by Parragon Books Ltd in 2014 and distributed by

Parragon Inc.
440 Park Avenue South, 13th Floor
New York, NY 10016
www.parragon.com

ISBN 978-1-4723-4155-6

Printed in China

Mickey's Puppy Pal

Read the story, then turn over the book
to read another story!

Mickey's Puppy Pal

Bath · New York · Cologne · Melbourne · Delhi
Hong Kong · Shenzhen · Singapore · Amsterdam

"Have a good time," called Mickey. Mr. Palmer was
leaving for an overnight trip, and he had asked Mickey
to take care of his pet shop while he was away.

"This will be a snap!" Mickey said.

"A snap!" repeated Mr. Palmer's pet parrot.

Mickey looked at the cuddly pets and colorful fish. They all seemed content ... all except one. A cute little puppy was whining and whimpering in such a sad way!

"Poor little fella," said Mickey. "I think what you need is some attention."

Mickey lifted the puppy from the kennel.
"Steady, boy," said Mickey. The lively puppy wriggled
free and raced over to the goldfish bowl for a drink.

"Watch out!" squawked the parrot.

He was too late—the bowl tumbled to the floor with a loud *crash!*

"Uh oh!" cried Mickey.

"Crash! Crash!" squealed the parrot, furiously flapping his wings.

"Gotcha!" Mickey caught the fish and put it in a new bowl.

Mickey put the puppy back into the kennel.
"Now you can't cause any more trouble."
Just then, Mickey heard the shop door open,
and in walked his first customer.

"Can I help you?" Mickey asked.

But before the customer could answer, the puppy escaped again and opened the door to a cage of mice.

"Eeek! I'll come back later," cried the customer. "Much later!" And with that, she raced for the door.

Mickey gathered up all the mice and put them back where they belonged.

"Don't worry, little guy," he said. "Someone will buy you, you'll see."

That night, the puppy howled at the top of his lungs.
Mickey covered his ears with a pillow, but it didn't help.

It wasn't long before the puppy got exactly
what he wanted—a cozy spot under the covers,
right next to Mickey!

When Mickey woke up the next morning,
the store was a mess! Worse still, he couldn't
find the puppy anywhere!

Mickey searched all over the shop for his little friend. Finally, he caught sight of a wriggling bag of fish food.

"There you are!" he said happily when the puppy
poked his head out of the bag. "I guess all you
wanted was some breakfast."

"Well," sighed Mickey, "I really should clean up the shop."
As he worked, the puppy trotted along beside him, helping out wherever he could.

"You may be a rascal," said Mickey, "but I'm getting used to having you around."

Mickey had just finished, when in walked Mr. Palmer.

"It looks like everything went smoothly," he said, handing Mickey his paycheck.

"Easy as pie," replied a very tired Mickey.

Mickey was about to leave when the puppy began
to howl and scratch at the door of his kennel.

"I'll miss you, too, little fella," said Mickey sadly.

Suddenly, Mickey thought of the perfect solution. He'd take the pup instead of the pay! Everybody was very happy—especially the parrot, who screeched, "And don't come back!"

"But what should I call you?" Mickey wondered.
Just then, he saw a newspaper headline:
NEW PICTURES OF PLANET PLUTO!
"That's it! I'll call you Pluto!" laughed Mickey.
Pluto gave his new master a big, wet kiss, and from
that day on, Mickey and Pluto were the best of friends.

The End

Now turn over the book
for another classic Disney tale!

Now turn over the book
for another classic Disney tale!

The End

Just then, Grandma Duck drove up. "I missed my cows
too much to stay on vacation," she explained.

"Hmph! I hope I never see another cow again as long
as I live!" Donald said grumpily.

"That's too bad," Grandma said. "Look what I bought you."

She handed everyone a box each. When they saw what was
inside, they began to laugh—even Donald. Inside each
box was a huge piece of milk chocolate, shaped just like a cow!

After their chores were finished, the gang trooped back
to the house and sat down for a rest on the front porch.

Mickey pulled Donald out of the can. "You've helped enough for today," he said, trying not to smile. "We'll finish milking Rosie."
Rosie stood contentedly while Mickey milked her, and then Huey, Dewey, and Louie easily led her to the box stall with her calf.

When Rosie saw Donald approaching, a sly glint came into her big, brown eyes. As soon as he got close enough, she gave a powerful kick—*thunk!*—and sent him flying through the air.

Donald landed—*splash!*—headfirst in a full milk can!

While Donald dripped and fumed, Mickey helped Huey, Dewey, and Louie catch Rosie. They tied her up and began to clean the barn.

But Donald wasn't about to quit yet. He grabbed an old milking stool and a bucket and marched toward Rosie.

"I'm going to milk this cow the old-fashioned way—by hand!" he declared.

"Oof!" Donald gasped as he climbed out.
He was covered with bits of mashed grain.
"Yuck!" Donald pulled pieces of wheat stalks
out of his sleeves and from under his hat.

With milk in his eyes, Donald couldn't see a thing.
He stumbled over hoses, boots, and milk cans, and
he bumped into doors. Finally, he put his foot straight
into a bucket, tripped, and fell into a feed bin.

Snap! One of the hoses suddenly came loose.
Milk sprayed everywhere, soaking Donald from
head to toe, and splashing in his eyes.

"Watch out, Unca Donald!" Huey shouted as Rosie dragged Donald through the barn. Donald's feet got tangled in the hoses that carried the milk to the storage tank.

"Now, that looks easy," he said. But when he tried it with Rosie, she pushed him over and started to run. "Whoa!" Donald shouted, grabbing her by the tail.

Spluttering and muttering, Donald finally managed
to get Rosie washed.

He watched Mickey and the boys hook the other cows
up to the milking machines.

Donald set the bucket down right behind Rosie.
Swish, swish! went Rosie's tail as she flicked it back and forth.
Plop! went the tail as she dipped it into the soapy water.
And *whap!* went the tail as Rosie smacked suds right
in Donald's face!

"You sure did!" Mickey agreed. Then he handed Donald a bucket of soapy water. "Now you need to wash her before she's milked."

Donald lugged the bucket into Rosie's stall. "Aw, phooey! Who ever heard of washing a cow?" he muttered.

Just then, Donald dashed into the barn with Rosie close
behind him. He raced into a milking stall with Rosie right
on his heels. Donald slipped out of the stall, slammed the door
shut, and leaned against it.

"Guess I showed her who's boss!" he said, wiping his forehead.

Meanwhile, Mickey and the nephews had led the little
calf into the barn and fed it from the bottle. Then they put
the calf in a straw-filled stall.

"When Donald gets Rosie into the barn, we'll milk her.
Then she can snuggle with her calf," Mickey told the boys.

"Come on ... move, you silly cow!" Donald ordered, trying to push Rosie aside. Rosie refused to budge, so Donald pushed again.

That made Rosie mad. Bellowing angrily, she pushed Donald back and began chasing him around the pasture!

"Grandma says to take Rosie's calf to the barn and help it drink from a bottle," Mickey said.

Donald tried to lead the calf in the direction of the barn, but Rosie blocked his way.

"I said, 'Here, cow!'" Donald yelled, stomping toward the big animal. Mickey, Huey, Dewey, and Louie hurried over to see what was happening.

There, next to the big cow, stood a little calf.

"Why, this must be Rosie and her new calf!" Mickey exclaimed. "Grandma mentioned them in her instructions."

Mickey and the boys found the cows drinking from the
farm pond. Mickey gave the largest one a gentle pat to
get her started toward the barn. The other cows followed.

Donald saw one last cow standing behind a big bale
of hay. "Here, cow! Here, cow!" he called. But the cow
wouldn't come.

Mickey read Grandma's list. "It says here to milk the cows in the morning, put them out to pasture to eat grass, and then take them to the barn for their evening milking."

"I knew that," Donald said. Whistling a cheerful tune, he headed for the pasture. Mickey followed with Huey, Dewey, and Louie.

"Grandma Duck left us lemonade—and plenty of instructions," said Mickey.

"Who needs instructions?" Donald replied. "I already know all about cows."

"Here we are at Grandma Duck's dairy farm," Donald said
to his nephews Huey, Dewey, and Louie one summer morning.
Mickey was with them, too.

They had all promised to take care of Grandma's cows while
she was away on vacation.

Fun on the Farm

PaRragon

Bath · New York · Cologne · Melbourne · Delhi
Hong Kong · Shenzhen · Singapore · Amsterdam

Disney
MICKEY
& FRIENDS
Fun on the Farm

Read the story, then turn over the book
to read another story!

This edition published by Parragon Books Ltd in 2014 and distributed by

Parragon Inc.
440 Park Avenue South, 13th Floor
New York, NY 10016
www.parragon.com

ISBN 978-1-4723-4155-6

Printed in China